KT-494-979

Ouch!

KT 0928810 4

KINGSTON UPON THAMES Libraries	
0928810 4	
BR JFF	PETERS
03-Aug-2009	£3.99
	KN

First published in 2008
by Wayland

This paperback edition published in 2009

Text copyright © David Orme 2008
Illustration copyright © Beccy Blake 2008

Wayland
338 Euston Road
London NW1 3BH

Wayland Australia
Hachette Children's Books
Level 17/207 Kent Street
Sydney, NSW 2000

The rights of David Orme to be identified as the Author
and Beccy Blake to be identified as the Illustrator of this Work have
been asserted by them in accordance with the Copyright, Designs and
Patents Act, 1988.

All rights reserved

Series Editor: Louise John
Editor: Katie Powell
Cover design: Paul Cherrill
Design: D.R.ink
Consultant: Shirley Bickler

A CIP catalogue record for this book is available from the British Library.

ISBN 9780750254588 (hbk)
ISBN 9780750254595 (pbk)

Printed in China

Wayland is a division of Hachette Children's Books,
an Hachette Livre UK Company

www.hachettelivre.co.uk

Ouch!

Written by David Orme
Illustrated by Beccy Blake

WAYLAND

Dad was hammering.

He hit his thumb with
the hammer.

"Ouch! That hurts!"

Mum put a bandage on
Dad's thumb.

"You need to be brave like me!" said Freddy.

Jess was playing in
the garden.

She was stung by a bee.

"Ouch! That hurts!"

"It's only a bee sting!"
said Freddy.

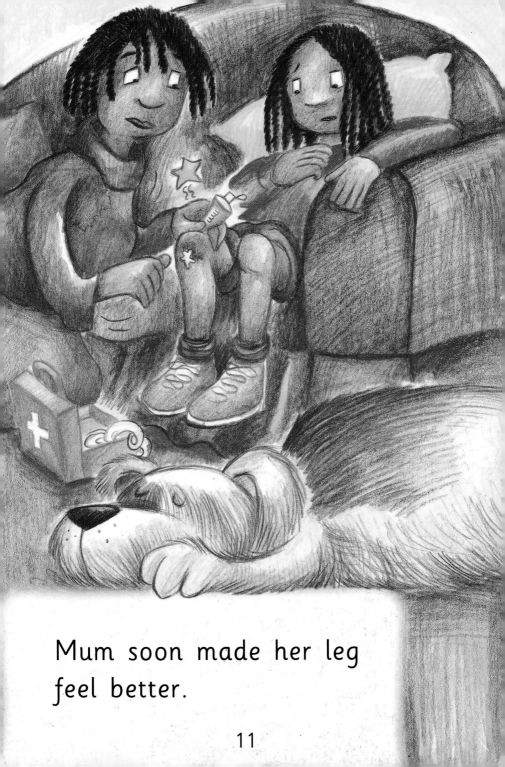

Mum soon made her leg
feel better.

Sam fell over and banged
his head.

He began to cry. Mum gave him a hug.

"Did that hurt?"
said Freddy.

"You need to be brave like me," he said.

"My leg hurts," said Jess.

"My thumb hurts,"
said Dad.

Sam's head still hurt.

Everyone felt very sad.

Mum put Sam down to play with his toys.

Freddy was playing, too.

Suddenly Sam hit Freddy with his hammer.

"Ouch! That hurts!"
said Freddy.

The family stopped
feeling sad.

They began
to laugh.

"You need to be brave
like us, Freddy!" they said.

START READING is a series of highly enjoyable books for beginner readers. They have been carefully graded to match the Book Bands widely used in schools. This enables readers to be sure they choose books that match their own reading ability.

The Bands are:

Pink / Band 1
Red / Band 2
Yellow / Band 3
Blue / Band 4
Green / Band 5
Orange / Band 6
Turquoise / Band 7
Purple / Band 8
Gold / Band 9

START READING books can be read independently or shared with an adult. They promote the enjoyment of reading through satisfying stories supported by fun illustrations.

David Orme lives in Hampshire, England. He taught for 18 years before becoming a full-time writer. Recent books are on subjects as varied as dragons and how to be a pop star!

Beccy Blake started drawing family life when she was about Freddy's age, and has never really stopped since. Her Granny had a dog like the one in this story and Freddy is very much like her little brothers, getting up to all sorts of mischief.